The People of the Sea

Published by Inhabit Media Inc. | www.inhabitmedia.com

Inhabit Media Inc.
(Iqaluit) P.O. Box 11125, Iqaluit, Nunavut, X0A 1H0
(Toronto) 191 Eglinton Ave. East, Suite 301, Toronto, Ontario, M4P 1K1

Editors: Elizabeth Issakiark
                Pelagie Owlijoot
                Neil Christopher
                Louise Flaherty

Art Director: Neil Christopher

We acknowledge the support of the Canada Council for the Arts for our publishing program.

This project was made possible in part by the Government of Canada.

ISBN: 978-1-77227-138-6

Printed in Canada

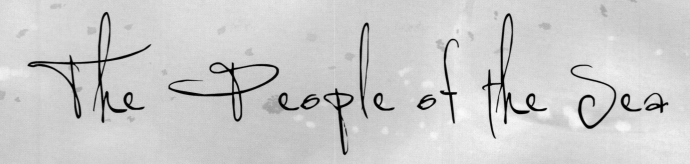

The People of the Sea

Told by

Donald Uluadluak

Illustrated by

Mike Motz

Dedication

Naming traditions and customs are an important part of Inuit culture. As such, this book is dedicated to the first boy who was named after Donald Uluadluak after Donald passed away—Raymond Uluadluak Ootoovak.

This book is also dedicated to all of Donald's grandchildren and great-grandchildren.

Introduction

Many years ago I met Donald Uluadluak when I travelled to Arviat to interview elders about traditional stories. Donald was a fantastic storyteller. He generously shared both personal experiences and folktales. He was very giving with his time and his knowledge.

Several years later, Donald contacted me about working on a book together. I remembered our first time working together and I was excited to work with him again. Donald explained that in his free time, he had been creating children's books about traditional Inuit skills, such as meat caching and Inuit games. It was his hope that these cultural skills and this knowledge would be passed on to the younger generation, and not forgotten.

After several interviews, I noticed that he had valuable personal experiences to share with us about dogs, and we worked with him to create a book called *Kamik: An Inuit Puppy Story*. This book received critical acclaim and award nominations in the south. It has also been well used in the North in both English and Inuktitut.

Several years later, Donald developed some health problems, and his daughter, Elizabeth Issakiark, began working with him to record his memories and knowledge. After Donald's passing, Elizabeth continued to work tirelessly to ensure that her father's final wishes would be honoured. The book you are holding is one of the results of Elizabeth's work, her love, and her respect for her father.

I am grateful to have known Donald, and to be working with Elizabeth and the rest of Donald's family.

—Neil Christopher
Iqaluit, Nunavut

Pronunciation Guide

There are a few Inuktitut words in this book that people not living in the North might have trouble with. Below, we offer a pronunciation guide and translations to assist those interested.

Arviat	ar-vee-at	This is the name of the community where Donald lived. In Inuktitut it means "place of bowhead whales."
Nunavut	new-na-voot	This is the name of the eastern Arctic territory in Canada. In Inuktitut it means "our land."
arnajuinnaq	arn-a-u-een-nawk	This is the term used in Arviat for the people of the sea.

Preface

My late father, Donald Uluadluak Sr., was the most humble, honest, kind, strong, fair, and, above all, respectful man. He believed in these qualities throughout his life. He was a leader and a strong promoter of education. He always used to say that he learned something new every day, either from books he read, new people he met, his family, friends, and colleagues, or the places he visited. He was very generous and willing to share his knowledge for the benefit of the younger generation. Our father was a "big man" with an even bigger heart! He found good in every person he met.

I am honoured to have continued working to finish the work he was not able to complete before he passed away. I am grateful that he believed in me to finish this work.

He was my hero, now my angel.

—Elizabeth Issakiark

What I am about to share is a true story.
It happened to me when I was a child.

This story takes place near Arviat, Nunavut, in 1940.

My two friends and I were playing down by the beach.
We were having fun looking for sculpins.

Suddenly, one of my friends pointed out
to sea and said, "Look at that!"
    There was a woman in the water,
looking at us.
    I was very close to her, only about
ten feet away.

This woman did not say anything, and she did not smile. She just watched us play. I remember that she was very beautiful, with pale skin and long, dark brown hair. Her hair almost looked like seaweed.

"Who are you?" I called out to the woman.

She did not respond. She just continued to watch us from where she floated in the water.

This woman was starting to frighten us, so we backed away from the shore and started running back to camp.

Our camp was very far away from the shore,
so we ran for a long time to get home.
    We could not wait to tell our families
what we had seen.

But, before we got to the tents, we forgot
why we were running back to camp.

21

A year passed before my friends and I remembered what we had seen in the sea that day.

When we told our parents and grandparents about the woman in the water, they had a name for her. They called her an *arnajuinnaq*. They told us she was one of the people of the sea.

We really did see an arnajuinnaq that day.
The three of us were just kids, but we
remembered that woman in the sea all
our lives.

Our parents told us that, in the past, people of the sea were easy to spot. But by the time I was a boy, they had become rare and were not often seen.

Donald Uluadluak

Donald Uluadluak was an elder from Arviat, Nunavut. He was born in Arviat and raised by his grandparents, when Inuit were nomadic and depended on animals for survival. He was an elder advisor for the Nunavut Department of Education for several years. After he retired, he began recording memories and recollections from his life to publish as books for future generations. *Kamik: An Inuit Puppy Story* is the first book to be based on these fond memories. He was passionate about teaching the younger generation so that they would in turn pass on the knowledge he shared.

A drawing by Donald Uluadluak depicting the woman he saw in the sea.

Iqaluit · Toronto